Cha
Of All the Money That E'er I Had

Author
Justin Colt Canterbury
*****

Editors
Justin Colt Canterbury
Nykyrian Salvatore
Archer Abernathy
*****

Artist
Justin Colt Canterbury
*****

You must take up an oar, and walk inland. Keep walking until someone mistakes that oar for a shovel.

That is where you will find peace.

For that is a place where no man has ever been troubled by the sea.

The saloon was dank, almost decrepit. It was heavenly compared to the memories she was attempting to drown away. At least the mead was good and strong, all you really need for the job. Even only slightly North of her cold ancestral home, the dark skinned sailor was met by a strong sense of alienation.

'Twas midnight when she arrived in port. The now slowly rising sun gave the establishment a warm glow that could just about make you think it welcoming.

She was the only of her ilk in the building, and a moment's glare was common. Even the cute, friendly bar maiden didn't seem to know what to make of her. *"And damned if it wasn't hot."* She thought, leaning and trying to relax at the bar.

It's not as if the distrust wasn't mutual. Despite being so close to familiar waters, the clientele of this establishment seemed particularly seedy. She couldn't help but wonder if this is what all Northerners were like. What's more, she couldn't quite make out if it was her skin or her grey and dark blue trimmed Navy uniform that warranted such reactions. She doubted either truly helped.

The patrons all quickly grew silent as the door of the tavern slammed open. She could hear firm, surprisingly light bootsteps enter, followed only by a single other much heavier and softer set. Obviously whoever it was drew quite a bit of attention, as the conversations of all the sailors never once continued.

With the stark silence, she could easily hear the pair move to the far table behind her to the left. Only one took a seat. In that moment, it seemed all the sailors stood at once. She genuinely couldn't tell if a fight was about to break out.

Her nerves only slightly calmed when the maiden seemed somewhat happy to see these people, and nearly rushed over to serve them. A drink could be heard pouring, a sip... and a loud clop of the tankard back onto the table. A low and somewhat harsh, but unmistakably feminine voice finally broke through the thick air, "I've one open spot."

In less than a moment, all voices seemed to raise at once. It was a mass of noises that could hardly be distinguished from one another.

"Take me!" A sailor said. "I'm one of the most loyal men you'll find in this hole." He reasoned.

"Been sailin' goin' on twelve years now..." Another started. "You don't want some inexperienced whelp do ye?"

"Enough!" The woman's voice shouted over the rambling. Again... silence. "I need *one* sailor, for a very important role. I can't just take any blunderbuss that spins me a tale. I expect to be here awhile."

She could hear what seemed to be a parchment and quill being set on the table. "Line up one at a time... instead of acting like children. Write your name and a short word about yourself, and let's us have a chat. Anyone not willing to do that, is free to leave now."

The sharp clank of some therons could be heard, and the bar maiden soon returned to view tucking what seemed like much more than a drink's pay into her blouse.

A scant few moseyed out of the building, and the maiden moved along to lock the door soon after them.

The Southern sailor remained silent, only holding her hand out the odd few times to refill her drink. The process continued behind her for what seemed at least an hour, likely longer.

The more she drank, the less she cared about whether or not anyone decided to notice her. Small talk erupted amongst the crowd during their wait. From time to time, she could even hear the woman chatting with the next in line. It all blurred together.

It was strange: A strong drink was usually a source of joy... This time was different. In her attempts to forget her troubles, she was only reminded of them. Isolated from everyone around her.

She still received looks of caution from those who came to the bar for one reason or another. She was essentially just waiting for one of them to start something.

Almost as if a vindication, she felt a large hand land on her left shoulder. In a split second: She grabbed, pushed the thumb in at it's base, and stood to twist the arm behind him.

"Whoa, whoa lass!" He cried, gaining passive attention from some of the others. "Twas a friendly gesture, a pat on the shoulder is all. No need to break it!"

In a blind rage, she nearly didn't even notice his plea. After a moment of catching the breath she hadn't realized she lost, she could tell he seemed sincere, and released her grip.

"Gods, if I'd known you'd have such an aversion, I'd 'ave said somethin' first." The man jested, regaining his footing.

While most seemed to almost ignore the exchange as standard fare, she was acutely aware of one set of yellow inhuman eyes peering at her. It was the woman everyone seemed so intent on being recruited by.

She'd seen members of the beast races before, many from her homeland were even like family. But this was the first time she'd seen anything so... fish-like. "*Any-**one***", she was sure to remind herself. The sight was so alien to her, she very nearly didn't even regard it as another person.

The woman had an almost leathery skin that was two different shades of maroon, with near black stripes decorating both her face and the tops of her clawed hands. Was her whole body like that? It was then she noticed a finned tail waving freely under the table.

The answer to her previous question was likely "yes", as it bore the same design. It was bizarre to see a head of short silver hair on a creature so otherworldly.

Those eyes never turned away from her in that moment. It was then she realized the woman was wearing what seemed to be an Imperial Navy coat and tricorn hat... A very old set, judging by it's deep blue coloration and golden trim.

It was odd, because the beast races weren't allowed into the Imperial ranks.

"How about I buy ye a drink?" The young sailor suddenly offered as the moment passed, tearing her attention from the strange woman.

She looked back, only to notice the woman had returned to her conversation with the most recent possible recruit. "No... Thank you."

After she returned to her seat, he sat down on the stool beside her.

"Look... To assuage any reasonable fears ye might have: It ain't like that. Ye just look like ye could use another." He explained.

"I appreciate that, but I'd rather just be left alone." She said with a diminishing tone.

The man held up his hands, preparing to elaborate. "Full transparency lass: Part of the reason I'm talkin' to ye, is because we're far enough South for some of the lads to recognize that coat yer wearin'."

"I assumed as much."

"Some of 'em worry ye might be on some stinkin' official business... But I've seen your type before." He said, leaning in a bit.

"And what type is that?" she replied, barely turning her head from the tankard.

"The type that wants to drown whatever shite they've seen as far away from any regular presence as humanly possible."

"I'd say that's about right." She confirmed.

"All I needed to hear, mate." Before getting up to leave, he placed a few therons on the counter, and slowly slid them over to her. "And uh... I insist on the drink."

As he walked away, she felt the tension that had been building since she walked into the saloon quickly ease.

The now very inebriated sailor couldn't tell how much time had passed. She let herself get a bit carried away after it was clear she likely wouldn't be the target of any sort of attack.

She certainly heard the commotion and rustling of the drafting behind her, but she could no longer make heads or tails of the information.

It soon got quiet, peaceful even. She'd finally almost forgotten why she was sitting in such a worn down place. She felt warm, like she could finally relax.

"That's quite the iron gut you've got there..." A woman's voice she could swear she recognized arose from behind.

Upon turning to look at the approaching figure: It was her, the woman everyone had been so enamored with. She wasn't sure when all the other sailors had left, even the stranger's companion wasn't present.

The creature continued approaching from behind with her hands behind her back. Her canter seemed almost... giddy. "What's someone with such a deep purse doing in a place like this?"

"Deep... purse?" She struggled to understand.

"You've got quite a few drinks in you, and those don't come quite so cheap these days." The woman toyed, as she leaned in closer.

A realization hit at that moment. "Have I been paying for my drinks?" She directed at the bar maiden, with a slight panic.

"No, ye haven't been for quite some time. I assumed ye must've meant to pay me when yer head had cleared." The maiden confirmed.

The sailor sprawled her arms over the bar with what little strength she could muster, feeling genuine remorse. "I'm... I am so sorry, I don't think..."

A familiar clawed hand slamming down onto the counter silenced her lamentation. "Don't mind it, I'll cover the lass' tab."

The woman lifted her hand, revealing a large stack of therons. This person had quite the silver tongue, and the money to make it golden.

Even in this state, the sailor could tell she would need to be a lot more mindful of whatever was going on here.

"Do *you* have pure intentions, paying for my drinks?" She managed to put together, despite her slurred speech.

"Not at all." The woman replied with a smirk.

She couldn't tell if they had a mutual understanding of that statement.

"What's your name, Navy woman?" the creature asked.

"Ki'Leena... My name is Ki'Leena Ka'Vir." She answered, returning to her drink.

"My name is Hammerhead..." the woman explained. "Captain Hammerhead."

It was even more bizarre to see her speak than it was to lay eyes on her for the first time. Every major articulation exposed her array of sharp teeth which were patterned in a way very different from what the shark-like appearance had Ki'Leena imagining.

"Do you know who I am, Ki'Leena?" The Captain wondered with a barely veiled grin. While she pondered the question, Hammerhead waved down the bar maiden for a drink of her own.

Ki'Leena did recognize the name, but she couldn't quite put her finger on it in the moment. Only vague notions of ill repute came to mind. "No." She answered plainly.

"Well..." Hammerhead began. "That's a pleasant change of pace, actually."

After having a few moments to reflect on the past hours and the timing of Hammerhead's "rescue", Ki'Leena took a more measured gaze at her. "So did you think my wits would never come back to me?"

"Pardon?" She toyed, donning a mask of innocence.

"Did you think I wouldn't notice that you instructed the bar maiden to stop asking me to pay for my drinks?" Ki'Leena affirmed.

The Captain's smile finally broke through. "You'd be amazed how many don't."

Something was off about the corners of her mouth, Ki'Leena could see it even in the dim light of the sunlit room. It was as if her lips didn't quite connect at those points.

"So Ki'Leena... What brings you to a bar in the middle of nowhere?" Hammerhead asked again with more earnest.

"I don't see any reason I should be honest with you." Ki'Leena redirected.

Though she didn't seem to mean to show it, Hammerhead's eyebrow perked ever so slightly. "That's fair. I suppose it's enough to know you're not still with the Imperial Navy."

"So he *was* one of yours." Ki'Leena accused.

"The boy?" Hammerhead confirmed, receiving a look that implied it was obvious. "No, it was just a bit of luck the lads here were just as worried about it as I was."

Hammerhead's drink was set down in front of her, and she took a gulp from it almost in that same moment. While she was busy, Ki'Leena took another quick look at the uniform she wore.

That was when she noticed an unmistakable bulge between her shoulder blades. Whatever was under there had to be at least half a foot long. As well, her sleeves were actually rolled up. Unlike the rest of her outfit, it's clear this coat was not made for her.

"Should I be worried about who you got that uniform from?" Ki'Leena inquired.

To her surprise, the captain fell into a short burst of laughter. "I don't make a sport of hunting regulars, if that's what you're implying." She explained. "This was just... a **special** occasion."

Ki'Leena began by taking a drink of her own. "So what do you want with me, and when were you planning on telling me you're a pirate?"

Hammerhead looking only a little shocked, commented, "You're a sharp one, aren't you?" With the flattery having no effect, she continued. "Alright, honesty then: I have a lead on a prize that ideally, won't even require any bloodshed to take. Ancient treasure, a once in a lifetime opportunity. What did you do in the Navy Ki'Leena, what was your station?"

"I was a captain." She answered plainly.

"A captain?" Hammerhead said with a much more visible measure of surprise. "At such a young age?"

"Our navy is still new, it's actually common."

"I doubt they let just any brat become a captain." Hammerhead observed, taking a more inquisitive tone.

"What does it matter?" Ki'Leena questioned.

"I don't just need a sailor, I need someone that can take command when I can't. Normally I prefer to take the helm myself, but I've a certain set of skills I can't take full advantage of chained to a wheel." she elaborated.

"What about your quartermaster?" Ki'Leena wondered.

"He's a great man, and an even better sailor. But the poor bastard's got no talent piloting a ship. He can help me get from one end of the sea to another, and bring us into port. But he lacks the quick wit required for combat." The Captain clarified.

"I thought you said 'no bloodshed'?" Ki'Leena prodded.

"I said 'ideally'." Hammerhead countered. "It's money, and I know for a fact I'm not the only one that's heard of it.

"Of course..." Ki'Leena scoffed under her breath.

"Excuse me?"

"It's always money with you people. I can't believe the first pirate I've met is actually proving the Empire right." Ki'Leena scorned more directly.

For the first time since the conversation started, Hammerhead took on a less than friendly tone. "Money has quite a few applications Navy woman. We all want it for different reasons."

"And what are your 'reasons'?" Ki'Leena asked in an accusatory manner.

"There's a part of me that might like to retire, leave all this behind. But I'm not just in it for the money, that's a means to an end."

"What end is that?" She wondered, a bit more genuinely curious.

"Whatever trite's been spreading back home: Forget it. Don't think us savages just because the Empire doesn't like us. You're smarter than that, have some self respect." The Captain began.

"I might be more willing to believe that if you'd actually explain it to me." Ki'Leena cut in.

Hammerhead turned to the sailor, the previous timbre returning to her voice. "I was getting to that." Though it didn't last, as the topic clearly made her more somber. "We're by no means the first to use the title of 'pirate', but we may be the first to band together and use it for a purpose."

"We target the source of our animosity, not the bystanders on the path to them. So unless you mean to tell me it was the Empire's positive influence that drove you from your homeland, I doubt we're as different as you seem to believe." She finished.

"So you're telling me your intentions are noble when you're robbing trade vessels?" Ki'Leena interrogated.

"I wouldn't call it that." Hammerhead agreed, drawing a look of perplexion from Ki'Leena.

"But when robbing a trade vessel threatens the livelihood of some Imperial bureaucrat because he's too incompetent to protect what he was trusted with, I know I'm hurting exactly who I intend to."

With that, Ki'Leena looked upon the stranger with a much clearer understanding. Something that seemed to be recognized by Hammerhead herself.

It wasn't some baser greed that drove this person, it was a desire for retribution. Something happened in her life and she wanted people to know there were consequences for it. These pirates weren't partaking in senseless violence, they were waging a surprisingly direct war.

"*I... I can respect that.*" Ki'Leena thought.

"I won't lie to you Ki'Leena, some pirates are exactly what you've heard. But we don't associate with the likes of them, despite how much the Empire claims otherwise." Hammerhead resolved. "I can promise you that much at least. But if you only want to stick around for this job, I'll understand."

"Why me?" Ki'Leena asked.

"You mean, 'why you and not one of the countless others'?" The Captain clarified. Ki'Leena nodded.

"I've had my eye on you since I walked in, that uniform caught my attention. I don't know if you're aware of it, but stories of the Na'La Navy reach very far North. Tales of razor edge battles fought in tight frozen rivers. You may not have heard of me Ki'Leena, but I *actually have* heard of you. And I need someone with your set of skills." Hammerhead illustrated.

That revelation caught the sailor off-guard.

"When you showed no interest in my arrival, it made me curious." Hammerhead continued. "It's not that I don't appreciate the admiration many have for me. But frankly I never really wanted it. I think I might like having someone on the crew who actually understands me, instead of someone who just wants to work for me."

"So Ki'Leena, what do you say?" The Captain propositioned. "...Or do you have somewhere else to be?

The dark skinned sailor stared into her tankard of mead, in which she could just barely make out her own reflection. Her senses finally returned, and she could once again smell the storm-weathered wood of the old building.

Ki'Leena guzzled the last of her drink, and spouted, "Cock it all."

She followed the pirate through the tavern's door, the mead finally losing its hold completely. The door gave way to a nearly blinding reveal of sunlight.

In that moment of crossing the threshold she didn't see, hear or even smell it, but she felt some presence to their right. Turning to look revealed Hammerhead's companion that Ki'Leena had lost track of. His green beast-like eyes were staring down at her, nearly the only thing visible in the shadow given his blackened coat of hair.

He pushed off the place he was leaning, and moved to follow directly behind Ki'Leena. An action that made her more than a little anxious.

"Saheel..." Hammerhead began from the front, waving her right hand as if to signal. "I approached *her*, there's no need to make our new recruit nervous."

His stout dark figure moved from behind and up to the Captain's left almost without a sound.

The island wasn't exactly large, and the township was even smaller. It wasn't long before they reached the docks, and it became readily apparent where they were headed.

Voices rang out in song and unison as they approached, the scale of the thing becoming difficult to ignore. The crewmen's performance of "Leave Her, Johnny" only added to the haunting sense of awe Ki'Leena experienced as she approached at the Captain's right and looked up at the massive structure of wood and steel before them.

This ship was enormous, the largest she'd ever seen. Something of this scale wouldn't exactly be capable of turning in the rivers back home. It wasn't as if she'd never seen any large man-made structure, the towers the Na'La construct for scouting certainly out pace this. But to see something of this size floating in the ocean... The main mast may almost reach the height of a watchtower.

The hull was made of a brilliant orange wood, with a trim painted an only slightly worn gold. There were so many gun ports on the starboard side alone, she had to wonder if it was even possible to use them all at once.

"One hundred and twenty four." Hammerhead abruptly commented.

"...What?" Ki'Leena inquired, trying to regain her train of thought.

"I saw you eyeing the gun ports. He has a total of one hundred and twenty four cannons. Four at the bow, eight at the stern, and fifty six on each broadside. That's of course not counting the few extras we store, just in case." The Captain's tone seemed more than a little pleased.

Hammerhead was happy to continue boasting. "His top speed reaches... eh... I'd say about ten knots. That sound right to you?" She finished, looking over at Saheel. His quick response was an affirming nod.

"I'd always heard these large vessels couldn't go any more than nine..." Ki'Leena added.

"Give or take. It depends on the wind, tack... And of course how the sea decides to behave that day. But aye, around ten." She finished with a devious smirk.

"Even so, that's true for ships moving at eight." Ki'Leena observed.

"If I had to wager: I'd say it's the lighter wood along with a ship of the line's large set of sails. We're quicker than most expect, but it does make us prone to splinters." The Captain reasoned.

"What's his name?" Ki'Leena questioned.

"The Acacia."

It was reaching high noon. Ki'Leena had been waiting at the pier while Hammerhead and Saheel directed the crew as they were moving cargo to and from the ship. It looked like a combination of a resupply and sales. Thankfully someone had left a chair nearby.

The Captain came down to the dock and got the attention of a crewman who'd just put a crate down. "Enderson, I want that chase cannon sorted before we raise anchor. You have everything you need now?"

"Aye Cap'n, he'll be set."

Hammerhead continued further down the pier like clockwork. Ki'Leena thought it nice to see she wasn't the sort to take a rest just because she wasn't doing the lifting. Quick and direct, not taking too much time to make certain all is in order. Just... letting her men do their jobs. Seemed to run as tight as a Navy crew.

She almost felt like she was back in the saloon. Ki'Leena was a new face, and these men made their suspicion no secret. Not that the sailor herself felt entirely confident about what she was doing there. Ki'Leena was still processing that she'd gone from completely lost to joining a band of pirates in a matter of hours.

A few moments after the work seemed to slow, she heard Hammerhead shouting up on the ship. Something about gathering everyone for a hearing on the main deck. It wasn't long before the Captain made her way down the ramp.

Hammerhead directed her gaze at Ki'Leena after scanning the pier. "Ka'Vir, follow me."

The ramp was... a bit more steep than Ki'Leena was used to, even just leading to the mid-hull doors. The Captain however had no issue strutting her way up each ridge of it, retaining her somewhat flamboyant canter.

Hammerhead led her through a tight grouping of crewmen, all staring as she passed. They eventually made their way to a set of stairs leading to the main deck.

Once at the top, Ki'Leena took pause. She was again struck by an impressive sight. There must've been hundreds of men scattered around the whole of the deck, many visible below thanks to the large open trap doors along the center. Even some members of differing beast races were scattered among them. Not a mutter could be heard after the duo stepped into view.

The Captain slowly moved away from Ki'Leena and began to pace between the openings.

"Men..." Hammerhead started in a softer tone than Ki'Leena had expected. "I'm about to ask much of you, I know that. But I would hope that I've earned enough of your trust by now that you'll be willing to do it for me."

She soon made her way back, turned towards the crew, and placed her hand on Ki'Leena's shoulder.

"This... is 'Ki'Leena Ka'Vir'." To her surprise, the odd crewman actually perked up at the sound of her name. "Put simply: She'll be doing my job whenever I'm indisposed. Both piloting and commanding."

That revelation drew some hushed responses from the men.

"We're meant to follow her orders Captain?" One called out from below.

"Yes, even Saheel will be under her command." Hammerhead answered.

"The lass is a complete stranger." He retorted.

"I've 'eard of her." Another noted.

A peer to his right turned with a bewildered expression on his face. "No you 'aven't."

The first, seeming offended, returned the look. "Yes I 'ave!"

"That's enough!" Hammerhead shouted over the banter. Her tone was more that of an annoyed mother than an angry officer. "Her name isn't exactly 'Richard Duncan'. But she *is* known, and she does have experience."

"I had an ol' mate..." Someone to their right piped up. "Ran a smugglin' operation down South... He was afraid o' you lass." He finished, pointing at Ki'Leena.

"She's a regular?" A concern could be heard from the crowd, followed by quite a few more worried comments she couldn't entirely make out.

"She *was* a regular." The Captain cut in. "Like many of you if I recall." Her response brought the lot back to silence.

"I don't expect you all to trust her, or even respect her. She'll have to earn that. I do however expect you to follow her orders. This ship still needs to sail. The moment she proves herself unworthy of the role, I'll throw her off the Acacia myself." Hammerhead finished.

The man who initially protested called up once more. "What do we call 'er Captain, what's her station? It'd be a mite confusin' if we called ye both 'captain'."

"Aye... that it would." Hammerhead confirmed, thinking for a moment. She turned and looked at Ki'Leena as a realization struck her.

"Shipmaster. From this point on until I say otherwise, Ki'Leena will be Shipmaster of the Acacia."

The Captain scanned the amassed crew a moment before ending her announcement. "Now get back to work!" She said, shooing them away by throwing her hands up. "We have a meeting in Port Saylen I don't intend to miss."

As they all scattered, Hammerhead turned back to Ki'Leena once more. "Like I said: We're headed for Port Saylen next. That's Northeast from here. Why don't you raise anchor and start us there, get familiar with the helm?"

"Yes Captain." Ki'Leena confirmed.

Hammerhead sauntered off towards the captain's cabin, waving her right hand in the air. "Welcome to the team, Navy woman!"

Ki'Leena was quite a bit more nervous about commanding the Acacia than she'd expected. It wasn't exactly her first time, but this wasn't exactly her crew. She actually grew up with a few of the men she served with in the Navy. But these were all strangers, and cutthroats at that.

And yet... they all patiently awaited her order. As she stood at the helm with Saheel to her right, this massive beast with a main deck the size of a main road in her home village was at her beckon call. All eyes were on her. Ki'Leena realized though: Something was missing.

"Saheel..." she said, turning to him with a hushed tone. "I won't sail under colors I don't know. Raise the flag."

"I want the closest man raising our colors, now!" He shouted, startling her. This was the first time she'd heard a single word come from his mouth.

To Ki'Leena's surprise, some measure of cheering actually erupted at the command.

A crewman repeated the order, calling up to the main mast. Another near the top on a platform carried it out, the blackened flag raising just into her view. The fabric was adorned with a white design – two crossed sabres underneath a humanoid skull with a sharp array of teeth.

Ki'Leena (getting a bit carried away with the reaction) shouted her own next order. "The Captain told me this vessel can reach ten knots... I'll pay for the next round of drinks if this crew can prove her honesty! I want every inch of sail on the wind!"

That certainly got a reaction, especially when a few men passed the message down. The roar was intoxicating. Within moments, the masts creaked as every sail was lowering to catch the current at their stern. The Acacia began to pull away from the pier faster than she'd expected.

It was... exhilarating.

But like any other, the moment passed.

The Acacia's crew had started another song as the ship skirted across the teal open ocean. Something about a woman named "Nancy". To pass the time, Ki'Leena guessed. An interesting tradition that she was aware of, but wasn't really necessary back home.

Saheel returned to the poop deck, taking an extended look at Ki'Leena as he walked up the stairs. "You look as if you're very hot in that outfit." He commented, rejoining her.

She wasn't surprised it was obvious. The heat back at port almost seemed too much to bear. Now they're traveling North, and the sun's been beating down on her the whole time. The tropical air was almost suffocating.

"I could lighten it up a bit but... I don't think I'd have to be wearing anything at all to be uncomfortable in this weather." Ki'Leena acknowledged. "I'll just have to get used to it."

"Even in Port Ha'Laalu, the air had a bite to it. I imagine your home must be quite cold." Saheel observed.

"It could get warm, enough to grow crops even. But nothing like this." Just saying it almost took all the breath she had.

"Is the sailing familiar, at least?" He inquired.

"Barely." She answered.

"Really?"

"The ship is similar, but the sailing methods are quite different. Then there's the open ocean..." Ki'Leena began, realizing she didn't quite know where to begin.

Saheel thankfully had an inclination. "What's different about our methods?"

"Well..." she started. "For one: The way the crew relays orders."

"How is it done in the South then, if not by calling to a mate?" Saheel wondered, his almost feline ears seeming to perk a bit.

"We use drums." Ki'Leena replied.

"Drums?"

"It's not as archaic as I'm sure it sounds." She explained. "When the captain issues an order for a particular speed for example, the closest drummer begins a specific rhythm that identifies that order. The rest of the drummers follow his lead, and the entire crew is directed almost at once."

"I imagine the smaller vessels makes that very efficient." Saheel noted.

"Exactly right." Ki'Leena continued. "We found that the simple sound was easier for every man to recognize quickly than a bunch of random callouts. There's a different beat or pattern for every essential, even firing cannons. And it's different for almost every ship."

"What is the purpose of that?"

"Identification." She answered. "There's no uniform code. But if you're familiar with a specific ship, you can know whether or not they're an ally by the sound alone."

"I'd wager that's useful in tight winding quarters."

"As is a healthy degree of paranoia." The Shipmaster added. "I'm so used to looking over my shoulder every few moments, it's odd to see an endless stretch of blue in every direction."

"Aye, you'll see everything coming long before it's a threat on these waters." Saheel agreed. "Ambushes are best done close to land."

Mere moments after Ki'Leena nodded in agreement, a sharp clack of boots on the deck below could be heard even over the singing. It wasn't long before Hammerhead's very distinct appearance could be seen at the bottom of the stairs on the starboard side.

"Saheel..." she called out with a surprisingly soft tone. "Why don't you continue on to port? I'd like to go over some things with the Shipmaster in my cabin."

"Aye Captain, I'll see it done."

Hammerhead had sat Ki'Leena down at her desk so that they could discuss how the Acacia is actually run day to day. Not necessarily because the Shipmaster would be taking over every single little duty, just so that she would be aware of all the mechanics and statistics that go into maintaining a ship of the line when performing her own.

They had been there for what must've been quite a few hours. Ki'Leena had spent some time piloting the Acacia towards its destination before their meeting, but now it looked as if the sun was beginning to set. The Captain poured two glasses of a drink Ki'Leena didn't recognize the name of. "Wine" she called it.

"It's four hundred men on a floating pile of wood for weeks on end, they tend to get a bit ancy." Hammerhead said. "It serves to drop anchor at every possible port and let their feet dry for a few days. Occasionally, we'll even stop by islands just to relax for awhile."

"Morale must be very important sailing the open seas like you do." Ki'Leena observed.

"Even more if you're sailing a pirate vessel." The Captain acknowledged. "We're all here for the same reason. But a lot of us have different motivations for it. If that operation starts to fall apart, there's not much else keeping us working together."

Hammerhead took a moment to sip from her strangely shaped glass, and then continued. "It helps to know your mates, remember there's another man under all that 'animalistic greed' when times are rough."

"Look..." Ki'Leena started, noticing the reference. "I'm sorry about that."

"It's fine, I'm used to it." Hammerhead abated, gazing down at the glass of wine as she shifted it around in her hand.

"That doesn't make it okay for me to do. I shouldn't have made assumptions like that." Ki'Leena affirmed.

The Captain's eyes were drawn to her at that. After a moment of veiled shock, Hammerhead let out a short chuckle.

"Did... I say something funny?" Ki'Leena wondered.

"No..." Hammerhead began, looking back down. "I just find it incredibly adorable how guilty you seem to feel over a simple misunderstanding."

Ki'Leena really didn't quite know how to take that insinuation. Did she mean it genuinely? Was it a friendly gesture, some turn of phrase she wasn't aware of?

Hammerhead could tell the comment had made her a bit uncomfortable. "Speaking of which, we should probably talk about how the Acacia actually makes money..."

"You're thieves, obviously." Ki'Leena indicated. Hammerhead gave what was almost a sort of bow from her relaxed position on the other side of the desk, holding her glass out as she tilted her head towards the Shipmaster.

Ki'Leena continued. "So... Is there some sort of procedure, or do you just take any ship that catches your eye?"

"Actually..." Hammerhead cut in, "we aren't even always going after ships. Sometimes it's plantations, the odd high value target and even some coastal raids."

"And the people?" Ki'Leena inquired.

"We don't slaughter them all for fun, if that's what you're asking." The Captain answered. "Really we'd prefer not to harm anyone. We threaten it sure, the greatest battles are the ones you never have to fight. But if we board a ship and they hand over what we ask, no one even needs to be touched."

"You're saying you're no more violent than simple burglars then?" Ki'Leena surmised.

"Against civilians... Yes, that actually is an apt comparison. However when it comes to navymen: Whoever's after whome is usually out for blood. It's best to act accordingly. We do make special exception for slavers, though."

Ki'Leena took a moment to finally drink some of the wine she'd been given, and collect some of her thoughts. This instance was made even longer by her surprise at how sweet it actually was.

Finally she said, "So how often do people actually surrender to you?"

"Almost every single time." Hammerhead replied.

At Ki'Leena's clear look of disbelief, the Captain elaborated. "Sailors are not usually treated well. Why do you think there are so many pirates? Merchant vessels pay a pittance, and the navy uses them like dogs."

Hammerhead sensed that her words resonated with Ki'Leena on some level, judging by the look on her face. She stood up to strike matches for the candles on her desk as the last scraps of sunlight slid out of the cabin.

After sitting back down, she proceeded. "Most of the time when we rob a vessel, half of the crew wants to leave with the cargo. I've been in more bar fights than I have battles atop the deck of a ship. And that's saying something, I fought in the war. Make no mistake: We get into some scraps, but it's nothing like the Empire tells it."

Ki'Leena was a bit confused by that last comment. "Which war?"

"The most recent one darling, the 'War of Tides'."

The Shipmaster had to wrack her brain at that. She knew about it, but the Captain just didn't seem old enough to take part in it. "But... that was forty years ago..." she pointed out.

"That's right." Hammerhead confirmed.

"... How old are you?" Ki'Leena wondered.

Hammerhead seemed to have to think about it for a moment. "Um... Somewhere in my sixties, I'd wager."

"You don't know?" The Shipmaster continued to question.

"My kind doesn't worry about birthdays so much. And those that do... Well, they tend to stop after one hundred or so." She explained.

"How long does your kind usually live?" Ki'Leena asked, now curious about these people she's realizing she knows almost nothing about.

"It varies." Hammerhead stated plainly. "I'll put it to you this way: *I'm* still in my prime."

Ki'Leena, unsure she wanted to try and process a life span like that in this moment, moved the conversation back on topic. "So what about non-Imperial or colonial vessels?"

"We don't really bother with them if we don't have to." Hammerhead replied.

"Why not?"

"Why should we?" Hammerhead retorted. "Most of us pirates take particular issue with the Empire. More often than not, they are why we do this. Independent merchants don't carry as many goods, so that's not exactly an incentive to go after them as well."

She continued. "I doubt other nation governments are much friendlier than the Empire's, but we don't know them as well. We already have enough of a problem with one crown breathing down our necks. So going after them would be more risk than we need."

"So you really are waging a war..." Ki'Leena noted.

"Caught that, did you?" Hammerhead praised, genuinely a bit impressed she picked up on it simply through hearing the strategy.

"Imperial sponsored merchants, coastal colonies, slavers... Instead of directly opposing an enemy with overwhelming numbers, you've taken to robbing them of their wealth. Sowing discontent, inspiring rebellion..."

"Destroying their rotten nation from within." Hammerhead confirmed.

At this point, neither of them were sure how long it had been. They'd both partook in quite a bit of Hammerhead's wine. The conversation had shifted back to the semantics of day-to-day operation.

"So what if there's an extended period between ports, or maybe things get a little tense before we make landfall?" Ki'Leena inquired.

"That's why it helps you're a fresh face... and easy on the eyes at that." Hammerhead's response wasn't exactly what the Shipmaster had expected, and she could only assume her anxiousness was becoming more obvious. "Mingle, maybe play a game with them. Or even share war stories, I only have so many of my own. Anything that lets them think of something other than the endless ocean for awhile should do the trick."

Ki'Leena smirked, the intoxication beginning to take over her mind. "Somehow I doubt I'm nearly as interesting as you, Captain."

Hammerhead dawned a playful grin at Ki'Leena's response. "Oh come now Ki'Leena..." she leaned in. "I for one find you **very** interesting."

The Shipmaster was taken aback by such a statement. "I... You do?" Hammerhead slowly stood up and began to waltz over to Ki'Leena while she stammered. "What could possibly be interesting about me?"

The Captain abruptly clasped her left hand on the back of Ki'Leena's chair, pushing it off of its front legs. It was at this moment the Shipmaster managed to grasp what her new captain had been insinuating this whole time.

Hammerhead placed her right hand on Ki'Leena's cheek, gently running her thumb back and forth over her lips as she stared into the dark skinned woman's ice blue eyes.

"There's quite a bit I find interesting about you, Ki'Leena."

The Shipmaster sat there stunned for what felt like an age. It's a forward approach she wasn't exactly expecting.

Hammerhead moved closer as she stood over the Shipmaster. "If you like, you could spend your nights in my cabin and we could talk more about it..."

With the look in Ki'Leena's eyes and the flushing of her soft cheeks, the Captain knew she was having the effect on the poor girl she desired.

"Besides..." Hammerhead tilted her head a bit, softening the gaze of her beast-like yellow eyes. "A lady like you shouldn't have to share lodging with hundreds of poorly kept men."

Ki'Leena was entirely unsure what to make of this gesture. She was flattered for certain, and it wasn't as if the sentiment wasn't at all mutual. She too found the Captain... "interesting". But something did feel wrong about it to her, almost like a betrayal. This notion was solidified by the pit in her stomach when she felt the thumb begin to slide into her agape mouth.

Hammerhead felt Ki'Leena's hand lightly grab hers, and pull it away from her face. Without a word, the rejection was clear. She was actually surprised by it as well.

"I'm..." the Captain began, drawing back and letting the chair rest back on all four legs. "I'm sorry, did I misread something? Did I make you feel uneasy?"

Ki'Leena was once again shocked, never expecting to see someone like Hammerhead be so genuinely apologetic.

"No, it's alright." She consoled, looking down with a slight smile and brushing her bangs out of her eyes.

The Shipmaster's expression soured as she was about to recount her reasoning. "I just..." Ki'Leena looked back up at Hammerhead. "Something happened recently, to someone I cared for deeply. It just didn't feel right."

"I see..." Hammerhead affirmed, taking her hand off of the chair entirely and stepping away.

"Well, the offer still stands for you to sleep in here. I still don't think you should have to spend your nights in the same room as the men." The Captain began explaining as she removed her coat.

The Shipmaster became distracted by what appeared to be a fin between her shoulder blades, explaining the bulge she noticed earlier. "I can set up some bedding on the floor for myself until we can get a hammock or something for you, I don't intend to make you uncomfortable."

Ki'Leena nearly didn't register the implication. "What? No... No that's not necessary. I can sleep on the floor for now."

Hammerhead turned to Ki'Leena while she removed her vest. "Now now: Just because you turned me down doesn't mean I'm gonna make you slum it on a wood floor."

"Well I don't really want to kick you out of your own bed either..." the Shipmaster countered. "It's big enough for the two of us, I don't mind sharing it until we figure something else out."

She couldn't help but notice the Captain smirking. "This isn't some ploy of yours, is it?" Ki'Leena accused.

Hammerhead, feigning offense replied with a hand on her chest. "Me? Of course not." However she quickly lost her grin and posture, returning to hanging up her vest with a somber tone. "I know what it's like to lose someone. I won't press."

The Captain turned back towards Ki'Leena as she loosened her belt, some of her smile returning. "I'm not that sort of gal either, forcing myself onto someone that doesn't want me."

"It's not that..." Ki'Leena let slip, causing Hammerhead to drop the trousers she was holding up with eyebrows perked.

The Captain stepped out of the discarded clothing and placed her right hand on her hip. "So you're tellin' me there's a chance?"

Hammerhead's slightly awkward reaction managed to derive a chuckle from Ki'Leena, pulling her from the lamentation she'd nearly returned to. When she looked back up at the beastial woman, she noticed her tail... It was swaying back and forth.

Ki'Leena didn't really intend to, but she ended up just staring at the now exposed pattern on her skin. The blackened stripes stood in stark contrast to the soft maroon fading into a shade of pink on the inner sides. It was so strange to her, but beautiful at the same time. She could still hardly believe a race of people like this existed.

Hammerhead bent down to match Ki'Leena's gaze. "Keep looking at me like that, and I'll have to take back what I said."

The Shipmaster shot up, realizing what she'd been doing. "I-I'm sorry, I didn't mean to..."

"It's alright." Hammerhead cut her off. "I know, you've never seen anyone quite like me before." She stood back up now that she had Ki'Leena's attention. "We've got about a week of ocean ahead of us. Why don't we save the anatomy lesson for later, lass?"

The trip to Port Saylen went surprisingly smoothly, not even a sign of adverse weather. As much as Ki'Leena might want to wish for some cooling rain, even she was well aware a storm could be disastrous on the open ocean. It goes without saying she wasn't exactly accustomed to the heat yet.

Their only real issue was some food supplies coming up short when the cook checked their stores. The plan was to buy some extra when they reach port, and see about correcting whatever the problem was.

Ki'Leena had mostly spent her days familiarizing herself with the Acacia. She'd need to know her way around well in case of emergency, and there was a lot more space to cover than she was used to.

The crew took some getting used to as well. They were still wary of her. Not that she could blame them, she hasn't really had a chance to prove herself worthy of the position she'd been handed. The crew attempted to be friendly, at least.

On the first morn of the trip, Saheel was forced to barge into the Captain's cabin. He seemed... agitated, at the sight of Ki'Leena and Hammerhead sharing a bed. He wasn't buying the Captain's plea of innocence, either. That was when the Shipmaster observed that the pair were quite candid with each other, with him pointing to her past of habitually lecherous behavior. She responded more like she'd been lectured by a good friend than a commanding officer that had just been blatantly disrespected.

They weren't the only two members of the Acacia's crew that seemed to have a history with one another. Many of these men were quite close. Everything from childhood friends, to freed slaves and their saviors.

Many people of countless races and creeds resided on this ship. Ki'Leena hadn't even heard of the places many of them were from before this voyage.

Hammerhead was a woman of her word as well. Outside of the odd playful gesture, she made no further attempts to seduce Ki'Leena. It was almost as if she felt guilty.

Despite the lingering distrust, the crew of the Acacia followed the Captain's order and showed proper courtesy to their new Shipmaster when addressed, and followed her orders the few times she needed to give them.

Even with their apprehension, Saheel's suspicion and Hammerhead's peculiar reaction to her... Ki'Leena felt welcome. It's a sensation she hadn't experienced for some time.

Hammerhead slowly opened the door of the captain's cabin, the morning light spilling through the crack and onto the bed where Ki'Leena still slept. Quietly, she made her way in and shut the door behind her.

She cautiously stepped up to the sleeping woman, almost afraid to wake her. The Captain sat down, stopping as she was leaning over.

Ki'Leena was sleeping on her left side, facing the door with her arm under the pillow. There was a blue beaded armlet on her bicep, strange that she'd wear something like that under her clothing. It was tightened nearly to its furthest extent, almost like it wasn't made for her.

The Captain didn't recognize the design, though it was obviously likely to be some momento from her home. She was so absorbed looking at this simple accessory, she almost overlooked just how fit the tribal woman was. Her features somehow straddled the line between strong and soft.

Captain Hammerhead had... "observed" quite a few women in her day from all over the world, but it would seem Southerners were of a different breed altogether. It was a collection of attributes never seen together anywhere else.

Even with them now closed, she had no trouble remembering the pale blue eyes behind her sharp features. It wasn't really common on someone with such dark skin, and an even darker head of hair.

She wasn't exactly looking above the eyes the last time she was this close to Ki'Leena. But now without the hat on, she was able to appreciate just how wild her hair truly was. Not quite tawny, but scarcely straight or fine. It was tightly braided in rows along the right side of her head while the rest was left to flow freely. It was a style complimented by the Shipmaster's thick eyebrows.

Hammerhead had almost forgotten what she came into the room to do... Ki'Leena was no strain on the eyes. She leaned in a bit more, and put her hand on the Shipmaster's shoulder.

"Ki'Leena..." Hammerhead softly called with a light shake. It yielded no response from the sleeping sailor.

Now she was beginning to worry. "Ki'Leena?" The Captain tried again, louder with a more vigorous shake. She let out a short delicate snore, putting Hammerhead at ease.

The smile on her face soon turned to a grin. The Captain pushed off of the bed, and stood up. She straightened her back, cleared her throat and yelled, "Ka'Vir, attention!"

Ki'Leena sprung up before her eyes even opened. She eventually managed it though, slowly turning her gaze over to her Captain who was doing her best not to laugh at the reaction.

"Well, if there was any doubt you really were a Navy woman..." Hammerhead commented.

"What's going on?" She struggled, rubbing her eyes with her fingers.

Hammerhead sat back down beside her."We're coming into Port Saylen. I thought you'd want to be awake to see the approach."

Ki'Leena was actually a bit touched by the thoughtfulness. This is a brand new experience for her, and she would like to see it. In fact it's the first time in her entire life she'll be seeing any place outside her Southern home's territory.

As they exited the cabin, one crew member was awfully interested in the sight of them together... And Saheel was right behind him, staring him down. When the man finally noticed, he gave the dour figure a meek smile. The Quartermaster slapped the back of his head, and pointed at a rope that needed securing.

When Ki'Leena finally joined Hammerhead next to the wheel, she saw it: Port Saylen. A modest city, but unlike anything she'd ever seen. The architecture followed all the same rules, but somehow managed to be so vastly different from anything back home. Squared brick structures with shingled triangular rooftops. The stone was brightly colored in all different shades.

The port was filled with ships of all shapes and sizes. Ki'Leena started to realize she can't even name most of these models... That's a problem she'd need to fix.

"Ki'Leena..." Hammerhead said, getting her attention. "Look there, southernmost pier." She finished, pointing to a brig at the end of the dock that boasted an impressive ram as they passed by. "It's the 'Steel Marrow', captained by 'Billy Bones'. Old friend of mine."

"Why 'Bones'?" The Shipmaster wondered.

"I gave him a hard time for looking like a dog, and it stuck." The Captain answered with a smirk.

Ki'Leena stared for a moment. "... What's a 'dog'?"

With that being the last thing she expected to hear come out of the sailor's mouth, Hammerhead turned to her in utter confusion.

It wasn't long before the Acacia docked at one of the larger piers. The bright yellow sailed ship of the line drew quite a bit of attention from a wide variety of people. Apparently it just "has that effect", or so Hammerhead claimed.

Port Saylen was a bustling trade town. Outdoor stalls were strewn throughout the crowded streets, animals Ki'Leena didn't recognize roamed freely.

Hammerhead stopped by one of the stands to pick up some loads for her flintlock pistol. As the owner was counting out her coin, she looked over at the Shipmaster. A pig had approached her... she had crouched down to pet it. The Captain couldn't help but smile at the sight.

She also realized she didn't actually recognize the two pistols Ki'Leena was carrying on the back of her belt... or the large knife, for that matter. It seemed everything about this woman puzzled her.

The odd familiar face could be made out in the masses of people walking the streets, clearly many members of the Acacia's crew had their own errands to run.

Eventually, the trio of Hammerhead, Saheel and Ki'Leena made their way to the "Bellyup Cafe". The "building" on the edge of town near the shore was nothing more than an overturned schooner hull with a door carved out of the starboard side.

"Yeah, it's a shithole." Hammerhead said, tilting her head over towards Ki'Leena. She'd been thinking it, but wasn't about to ignore the ingenuity.

"But it's one of the only bars in town, and where Billy said he'd be spending his days to wait for us."

"What did you say about my face!?" The trio could hear a gruff voice shout upon their entry. The exclamation was quickly followed by the sharp crack of a bottle breaking, likely over some poor sod's head.

As they passed the threshold and the door shut behind them, said likely receiver was being tossed onto a table.

"You think my mug is ugly... Yer own mother will disown you when I'm through!" The voice growled again.

Ki'Leena could now see the source of the verbal lashing, and it was a mountain of a beast man. He had fine grey hair, not too dissimilar from the coat Saheel bore. However where she could draw comparisons between the Quartermaster's appearance and felines, the only similarities this man had to anything she knew were the Na'Sakka back home.

Yet his features were almost entirely different. Small sharp ears and a face that almost appeared to droop. He **was** ugly, and was done no favor by the long scarred cut stretching from the top right of his forehead down to his left cheek. She couldn't imagine what kind of fool a person would have to be to tell him that.

As the bloody and battered sailor attempted to regain his footing, the man grabbed him by the collar of his shirt. One stiff strike was all it took to finally knock him out cold.

His victim now lying helpless on the floor, the man pulled out his knife and began carving a line across the sailor's face not unlike his own scar.

"Now now... Keep your bloomers on, Billy." Hammerhead cut in, getting the man's attention.

"Hammerhead!" He exclaimed, donning a surprisingly friendly smile. Billy immediately ceased what he was doing, and stood to greet the Captain with a vigorous handshake. "Well, if you aren't the catch o' the day!"

"Very funny, Billy." She jided, returning the gesture.

After it ended, Billy rested his hands on his hips. "What's it been, two years? How in blazes have you been?"

"Haven't you heard? There's plenty of tales being spun about you." Hammerhead replied.

"Aye..." Billy started, a mischievious grin crawling across his face. "But I'd like to hear it from the horse's mouth. Or, well..."

"Make another jape and I'll geld you." The Captain interrupted, sharing his expression.

Billy Bones met the comeback with a loud, guttural laugh.

The four of them were sat at a table, Billy bought them all a round of ale. This drink Ki'Leena wasn't keen on, but alcohol was a mite too expensive to be turning down the gesture of kindness. She'd have to politely decline the next one.

Hammerhead and her compatriots sat with her in the center, Saheel and Ki'Leena were to her left and right respectively. Her old friend was across the table from them.

"So... Who's the new girl?" Billy wondered, looking at Hammerhead and nodding towards Ki'Leena.

The Captain put a hand on her shoulder. "This is my Shipmaster, 'Ki'Leena Ka'Vir'."

"Shipmaster eh? How long has she been sailing with you?" He wondered.

"About a week now." Hammerhead answered.

"Huh..." Billy lightly exasperated before turning his attention to Ki'Leena. "She try to bed you yet?"

Ki'Leena was a bit flustered by the question, though she tried not to let it show. It's not as if he was wrong.

"Come now, who do you take me for?" The Captain countered, pretending to be offended by the accusation.

"Hammerhead, 'Mother of Pirates', 'Cougar of the Crimson Sea'. Pick one." He listed.

"It's 'Tiger'." Hammerhead corrected with a smirk.

"I know what I said." Bones upheld.

"Billy, I don't berate you about *your* carnal habits." The Captain protested.

"I don't hire the people I sleep with. Not for my crew, anyway. You're gonna make her mates jealous." He finished, wagging his finger at her.

"Alright fine: I tried, and I failed. Happy?" Hammerhead admitted.

Billy looked over at Saheel. "I didn't believe it either." He confirmed.

Ki'Leena was diving into her mug at this point, glad she seemed to be ignored by the conversation.

"Is it really that hard to believe I can't bed *every* woman on the Crimson Sea?" She reasoned, prompting Billy to turn back to Saheel.

"Then why do I find her under your sheets each morning?" The Quartermaster accused, causing Billy to shift his gaze once again.

"It's temporary!" Hammerhead finally shouted. "I didn't want her to have to sleep in the crew's quarters." She finished, now scratching the skirt of her tankard.

Billy turned to Saheel one last time. "By the Gods, I think she's tellin' the truth."

"Aye, that's because I am, git." She confirmed with a glare.

"Is that why you're so touchy about it, because you turned up the ol' charm and blundered it?" Billy's comment caused Saheel to let out the first laugh Ki'Leena had ever heard from him. "That must've been mighty awkward for you."

"Would you just drop it, ya lobcock?" Hammerhead sighed, attempting to change the subject.

"Alright, alright." Billy conceded, signaling for a waitress to refill their drinks. "Never change, Hammerhead."

As the maiden approached her mug, Ki'Leena gestured to stop her. "No... No thank you." She started, looking towards Billy. "I appreciate it, but I don't need any more."

"What's wrong lass, would you prefer somethin' else?" He kindly wondered.

After a moment of thought, she agreed. "Actually yes, some mead if they have it? A taste of home could be nice."

Billy gave the waitress a confirming nod. After she left, he continued the conversation. "So why'd you hire her, then?" He directed at Hammerhead.

"She's from the South, captained her own vessel down there." Hammerhead explained. "On top of having an extra head to fill in for me, she's experienced navigating icy rivers and such. Your letter mentioned the North, I thought her skills might prove useful."

"Aye, I can see that." Billy agreed, stroking his chin with the hand he was resting on. "You have any combat experience, Ms. Ka'Vir?"

Hammerhead turned her full attention over to Ki'Leena, crossing her legs as she leaned back to relax on the furthest arm of her chair. Clearly she was awaiting to be regaled with the details herself.

Ki'Leena took a moment to gather her thoughts, it was difficult to decide where to start.

"I was number seventeen of the first six hundred members of the Na'La tribe to be accepted into the Southern branch of the Imperial Navy. I was the tenth to earn the rank of 'captain'."

Billy now leaned back in his own seat, crossing his arms. He seemed to be taking a more keen interest in what she had to say as the waitress returned to fill her mug with mead.

After taking a swig of the familiar aromatic drink, she continued. "Being the daughter of a chief, I was expected to take part in the defense of our home. At the time, the formation of our Navy was the most important part of that aim.

I was also trained in tomahawk and knife combat from an early age, along with hunting and tracking skills. The chief of our fellow Na'Sakka tribe decided to pass his skills onto me, alongside his own daughter."

"Those are all pretty words, princess. But did you ever have cause to actually use those skills?" Hammerhead interjected.

"I was getting to that." Ki'Leena responded. "Hunting is a part of daily life in my homeland. At least it is for those expected to supply meat and hides to the tribe. Everyone had their own role to play, mine was protector and provider.

During my time as captain of the ICV Black Thunder, we sank thirty-eight vessels. All criminals of some sort, usually attempting to circumvent the Empire using our channels."

"Pirates." Saheel noted, receiving a nod from Ki'Leena.

"Twelve of them fared well enough for a boarding." She explained.

"In both Na'La and Na'Sakka, it's customary to behead those who commit grave offenses against the tribe as a mark of shame. I've personally taken the heads of forty six such people. Five of them were from the captains of pirate vessels." Ki'Leena concluded.

"And here I was worried you picked up some timid little sweetheart." Billy jested, turning to Hammerhead.

"I was beginning to worry myself." The Captain concurred.

Ki'Leena felt a pit grow in her stomach at the realization of how her past sounded to others. Even among infamous pirates, it seemed her deeds were particularly noteworthy.

"It's not as if I enjoyed doing it all." The Shipmaster defended.

"We never implied you did, lass." Billy consoled. "But it's certainly not the tale I was expecting from the woman that was too afraid to even speak a few moments ago."

Hammerhead could tell the topic was souring Ki'Leena's mood. "We know better than most a little brutality can solve a lot of problems before they start."

Her words however didn't seem much of a comfort to her new Shipmaster, so she opted to change the subject. "So, Billy..." she began, getting his attention. "When were you planning to tell me about that lead you found?"

"When I was finished prying into your business." He answered. Hammerhead was obviously waiting for an explanation, and Billy didn't intend to make her do it any longer. "From what I heard, the legend goes, 'Where honor inspires feud.' You can see why I guessed that meant our intense friends up North."

"That's it?" Hammerhead questioned.

"What do you mean 'that's it'? That's more than you gave me." Billy compared.

"Look..." Hammerhead started, holding up her hands and leaving the relaxed posture she'd had. "It's not like I expected a miracle. But 'North' doesn't quite narrow down the search."

"No... But it *does* point us to the people we probably *should* be asking about it."

The Captain looked lost in thought for a moment as she leaned forward onto her elbows. "Where exactly did you get this information?"

Billy, for the first time since the conversation started, actually hesitated to answer.

"*Billy*..." Hammerhead groaned.

"Look... Jorge got in touch with a historian in Sherwood that confirmed the existence of the legend." The pirate attempted to persuade. Hammerhead's expression was unchanging. "I paid a man in Sar Variner for the information."

"Was this man in a bar?" The Captain interrogated.

"Yes." Billy admitted.

"Was the amount you paid him enough for another drink?" She pushed further.

Billy sighed before answering. "Yes... But I've paid more for worse tips."

Hammerhead shoved her face into her hands.

Bones outstretched an arm, attempting to soften the blow. "Like I said, it's a real legend. It's not like I didn't check before I wrote you."

The Captain shot a look up at him.

"This could be a bust, I know that. So I'll cover the expenses up to Tengei territory." He negotiated.

Hammerhead took her hands off of her face, and leaned on her arms. "You'll cover the three week expenses of two other ships?" Her clarification seemed to stun Billy. "Did you forget Jorge would be coming with us?"

"I'll *find* the money to pay you both." Billy reiterated, managing to quell Hammerhead's clearly growing frustration.

"What makes you so sure the legend is talking about the Tengei?" She asked.

"It's talking about a feuding, honor-bound culture. Sounds like them to me." He reasoned.

"Billy, that describes the Elves too." Hammerhead observed.

"They're not feuding with each other..." Billy countered.

"They're feuding with the Tengei, *constantly*. And it's always over some old tradition or grievance." She pointed out.

Billy gestured a finger towards her as the point dawned on him. "... *Fuck*."

He leaned back onto the right arm of his chair, and rested his hand over his mouth while he took a moment to think. It looked as if a notion struck him just before he piped up again.

"Why don't we *start* with the Tengei? It'll be the harder trip anyway. Then we check around Elven territory. If that doesn't work out, we can get in touch with that historian Jorge knows. As we make some coin along the way, I can work on paying you both what I owe for the mistake." Billy offered.

Hammerhead considered the proposition for a moment before answering. "Don't worry about paying for our search in Tengei territory. I have an... old friend I wouldn't mind visiting in Ten Sekai."

"What about Jorge's expenses?" Billy wondered.

"He's a mutual friend. Trust me, Jorge would like to see him too." She assuaged.

"It's settled then!" Billy exclaimed, slapping the table's top.

Hammerhead, Saheel and Billy raised their drinks in toast, hesitantly joined by Ki'Leena. With a stiff swig, the deal was sealed.

It wasn't long after an agreement was reached before the newfound fleet set out together. They spent only a day at Port Saylen to let the Acacia's crew rest their feet on dry land. The plan was to take a more extended rest at Sherwood, the coastal Imperial city where they were to meet up with a man by the name of Jorge Gibson. The voyage was like to take them another week on the open seas.

Currently, it was the night of the first day out. Ki'Leena had just relieved Hammerhead of the helm when a passing crew member got the Captain's attention to ask a question.

"How'd ye meet Billy anyway, Cap'n?"

Hammerhead observed the small group around her, and pulled out one of the chairs near the base of the main mast. "Take a break boys, the Acacia'll hold." She prompted, before sitting down and getting comfortable with the chair's back in front of her. "This one may be on the lengthy side."

It wasn't long before a fair sized collection of crewmen had amassed around her. Ki'Leena was actually a bit surprised to see just how interested they actually were to hear a story from the Captain. This was clearly a sort of event to them.

Once they were all settled, Hammerhead began her tale.

"It was years back... Feels like a lifetime on nights like this. Most of the men walking these decks today hadn't even heard my name. Billy was already captain of the Steel Marrow when he started making rounds to Aussan. It was nothing more than a modest trade brig back then. Made most of his coin ferrying passengers and cargo.

Not that he had much of the former. Most Imperials were hesitant to trade with a freeman, let alone take up lodging with one for weeks at a time. Aussan was one of the few places a man like him could go to be treated as an equal among his peers. We paid him fair for his hauls, and he would always have a place to rest his weary head for a few days.

But not everyone liked the idea of any man having the right to earn his way."

The Captain's description alone had members of her audience scoffing. "Imperials." One muttered.

"Aye, Imperials. Even members of the Council made their disdain for places like Aussan no secret. A 'necessary evil' they called it, returning land to those who rightfully owned it. How dare some 'beast' lay claim to 'Imperial territory'.

Well unfortunately for them, a few Imperial Navy captains and their crews took the rhetoric just a bit too seriously. The daft bastards decided to put together a little fleet and take back what was 'theirs', starting with Aussan. A move so stupid, it could've reignited the war."

"Was the Council backin' 'em?" A crewman asked.

"No... Not officially, anyway. Anything beyond that is pure speculation I'm afraid."

"Wouldn't surprise me one jot, seems like the sort of underhanded t'ing they'd get up to."

"You might be right. But guessing at what the likes of them might've done a quarter generation past won't do us any good now." Hammerhead's sentiment looked to resonate with them, as many nodded in agreement.

"When those ships appeared on the horizon, I knew what it meant. There was no way in hell the Imperial Council sent ships to protect *us*. We were on our own.

The cheeky gits sent a messenger, demanding that I and the rest of the 'lesser men' vacate the island and leave our armaments on the beach. We hogtied the fool and threw him in a cell.

Me, the Acacia and her crew were the only real defense the island had at this point. There were a few ex-Navymen in the fort, but they could only do so much. We were the only thing standing between Aussan and a few hundred self righteous jackanapes.

... Until Billy saw us leavin' port without 'im."

The crew seemed mighty pleased with that implication, almost as if they knew what was coming next based on the idea alone.

"Way I hear it: That man walked straight up to the harbormaster, bought as many cannons and as much ammo as he had therons, and had his crew load and ready every single one onto the Steel Marrow. When other captains caught on to what he was planning, they followed right behind him.

An armada of traders sank three Navy frigates that day."

Ki'Leena was a bit surprised to see that some applause actually arose at that.

"We didn't pay them the kindness of simply being taken by the depths, we had something else in mind. We disabled and boarded every one of those ships with an objective. There were so many of us, it wasn't hard to take most of the crews captive.

Not that the plan meant much to Billy once we reached the flagship. I can't say I blame him though. After all, the captain did give him that scar across his face.

As thanks, Billy lopped the sod's head off where he stood." She illustrated with a hand gesture across her neck.

"When we were through, we had hundreds of prisoners. So we got to thinkin'...

We decided to drag that 'messenger' out of his cage. We judged and hanged every single man we had while he watched. Then we sailed to the nearest Imperial port and threw him overboard. I'm thinkin' we got the message across.

That's not just the story of how I met Billy... That's how the Republic of the Coast was born."

It was later in the night and the main deck of the Acacia had long since fallen quiet. Captain Hammerhead turned in for the night some hours after her tale.

It was only Ki'Leena at the helm and Saheel who was running final checks on the rigging before he went off to sleep himself.

Ki'Leena had begun to take the ship through a set of towering islands some leagues from the much more modest isle Port Saylen was built on. She'd been advised it was the shortest route to Sherwood, so she took it seeing as the Captain's meeting was like to be somewhat urgent. The Shipmaster guessed that a pirate staying settled in an Imperial controlled port city would have to be a risky venture.

A few times towards the end of the lull, Ki'Leena noticed the Quartermaster stand up on the railing of the starboard side and sniff the air with only a few moments between. On the fourth and final time, he took a bit longer scanning their surroundings before stopping, and suddenly bolting in her direction.

"Shipmaster!" He barely whispered as he moved up the stairs to her. "I smell powder on the wind from the South, but I can't see them yet."

Ki'Leena locked the wheel, and moved to the starboard side drawing her old spyglass from a pouch on her belt. Only the sea towards the bow and stern had open channels on either side of the island to the South. She first turned her attention past the bow, taking her time to look for any broken pattern amongst the stars and waves.

With no luck, she turned her attention to the opening on the stern. Again, nothing. She gave it some thought as she peered through the telescope: The wind was at their back, so it's most likely whoever Saheel caught the scent of was tailing them... And this channel is perfect for an ambush.

She lowerd the sight, and turned to him. "Start waking the crew, order them to simultaneously bring us to a full stop, and ready all cannons."

"Aye Shipmaster." He confirmed, and immediately started to move towards the stairs.

Ki'Leena stopped him just as he did. "Hand me your mirror."

The Quartermaster quickly removed it from his pocket and placed it down into her outstretched left hand, then returned to his task. She moved over to the port side, where the Steel Marrow followed closely behind. She angled the mirror to catch the moonlight, swaying it back and forth in her hand. Before long, she received a similar signal in return.

It wasn't long before a scattering of men started scouring the deck before her, passing commands along to each other in hushed tones. One had to shoo his mate away from attempting to light a lantern. Ki'Leena returned to the wheel and unlocked it. As the crew began to raise the sails, she spun it to her right, turning the Acacia starboard and exposing both broadsides to each open channel.

As the ship of the line came to a slow, the Steel Marrow began to approach their stern. Saheel had been readying a boat with some help and sent a crewman off in it, clearly intending to explain the situation to Billy without shouting from the deck. Ki'Leena locked the wheel once more and began looking to starboard through her spyglass.

As some crewmen came up to the poop deck, "Hey... you!" The Shipmaster called, catching one of them by the arm. "Port side, watch for ships." The man confirmed with a nod.

Saheel soon joined her while she watched, the dread of something she couldn't spot in miles of open ocean in the middle of the night creeping up on her. She began to wonder if she'd need to pass off the duty to someone more experienced... just before she saw it.

Creeping around the bend of the southern island was a distinct bowsprit and sail. "Starboard side, one frigate to the southwest." She relayed.

"Just one?" He wondered. "That doesn't make much sense. Any single ship that size would know they're out gunned long before we noticed them."

"I agree." Ki'Leena confirmed, unable to make sense of the logic.

In the quiet while they thought, the messenger returned and she could hear his boat being hauled back up.

"Can you see their colors yet?" Saheel asked, just before the opportunity actually arose.

It took her a moment to make it out in the scrap of moonlight. "Red..." she struggled.

"What pattern?"

"There isn't one, it's just red." Ki'Leena clarified.

"Bloody Reds..." Saheel noted, nearly under his breath.

"What?" She questioned, unfamiliar with the term.

"Pirates who offer no quarter." He explained.

With that, memories of the first conversation she had with Hammerhead came flooding back to her. A description of pirates that were every bit the savage raiders Imperial propaganda claimed them to be. "*But we don't associate with the likes of them...*" she said. Ki'Leena thought it a likely euphemism for "*they're enemies of the Republic of the Coast*".

Ki'Leena continued to watch the ship as it began turning towards them. "So they mean to attack us"

"If their cannons are loaded, that seems likely." Saheel confirmed.

"Crewman..." She directed at the port side. "Have any ships appeared?"

"No, Shipmaster." He replied.

Ki'Leena lowered the spyglass once more, and turned to Saheel. "I just don't understand what their plan is, this doesn't seem right."

"Something certainly seems off." The Quartermaster agreed.

Ki'Leena took a moment to breathe, and to think. She gazed past Saheel, staring at the rolling forest covered hills of the island to their bow.

"Gunpowder to the South..." She thought, a nearly forgotten battle returning to her mind in that moment. The Shipmaster took a more focused look at the elevation and tree cover it boasted, the cliff... "Loose the sails, full speed!" She shouted, startling Saheel who'd been wracking his own mind.

Ki'Leena ran back to the rear of the ship. Looking over the edge, she could see Billy at the helm. He had brought his own stern to theirs. "Billy!" She called, getting his very surprised attention. "Full speed forward, then move to the edge of the southern isle!"

"Aye!" Billy shouted back.

Ki'Leena ran back to the wheel as the canvas finished unfurling, unlocking it the moment she made contact. In the distance, she could hear what sounded like thunder. She couldn't see it due to the sails, but she knew what it was.

"Brace for impact!" The Shipmaster ordered, prompting the entire crew to duck for cover.

Not even seconds following, shots whizzed over their heads as no small amount of holes appeared in the Acacia's top main sail. As Ki'Leena looked back up, a screaming figure came plummeting from the mast. A missing leg was the least concern as his body buffeted the deck with a dull, booming thud.

She had no time to lament the loss however, as the ship was careening towards the cliff face. Once more, Ki'Leena spun the wheel as far as she could towards starboard. The Acacia was a fair degree more nimble than she had anticipated, allowing them to clear with ease.

"Port to starboard, prepare to fire!" The Shipmaster shouted over the main deck, with the crew relaying her order down the line.

The men on the port side began moving their boxes of ammunition to assist their mates across from them that were preparing to fire. The Steel Marrow seemingly managed to avoid the barrage (or at least make it through mostly unscathed), and was following close behind. The Bloody Red frigate was actually turning away, likely to avoid the longer range of the ship of the line they hadn't expected to launch such a decisive counter attack.

Though it's not as if they didn't plan for such a maneuver. This became obvious once the rapid cracking of grenades began rolling above their heads, and shrapnel was raining down on them. Yelps and wales rang out across the deck, confirming its effectiveness.

"Now would probably be a good time to wake the Captain!" Ki'Leena yelled at Saheel over the bombing.

"I woke her right after the crew, Shipmaster!" He explained.

Ki'Leena wanted to inquire further, but they were nearly in range of their target, and the dropping of grenades had nearly ceased. It was in that moment Hammerhead finally sauntered out of her cabin with a canter that didn't quite reflect the danger of the frequently spreading shrapnel.

"Starboard ready!" Ki'Leena called.

"Ready to fire, Shipmaster!" She heard a crewman respond.

"Fire!"

The sound was unlike anything she'd ever heard before. The deafening roar made its presence known with a vigorous rumbling that persisted long after she stopped being able to hear it. In the distance through a thick plume of white smoke she could make out the mizzen mast of the Bloody Red frigate tipping over.

As soon as the sound returned to her ears, she called out to anyone that shared her status. "Starboard side, reload! Rope men, to stern and starboard! Any man with hands free, take up a rifle and join them!"

After Ki'Leena finished her order, she looked up to observe the state of the main mast and sails. Hammerhead was there, hanging from the side facing starboard. She had this smile on her face... it almost seemed to break past the corners of her mouth.

The Shipmaster had already started the Acacia towards the frigate by the time the crewmen she called for found their new post. They were lucky to not be going completely against the wind while they were under the cliff, the wind currents flowing around the island mitigated the effect of their poor tack. Now though, their sails were catching the breeze proper once more. Even with a damaged sail, a frigate with a missing mast had no chance of escape.

"Shipmaster, we'll be in the line of fire of those cannons on the ridge!" A crewman shouted.

"If I see one hapless jolterhead try to stop this ship, I'll throw them overboard myself!" Hammerhead threatened, making her presence known to every man in earshot. "Those hooks better be tossed when we get in range!"

"Riflemen, fire on anyone that tries to cut a line or raise a barrel!" Ki'Leena commanded.

The Acacia drew ever closer to the frigate, and it was attempting to bring its port broadside around. But just as Hammerhead boasted, the golden sailed vessel was a fair bit quicker than they seemed to expect.

As the starboard side drew close, the rope men began slinging their hooks at the Bloody Red frigate. They did their damnest to bring about a mutual demise, but the enemy crew fired their cannons mere moments too late to land a critical blow on the Acacia. Within seconds they had been surpassed, their frigate pulled the lines taught and was being dragged by the ship of the line.

A distant roar cried out shortly before landing where the Acacia used to be. The result was the Bloody Red frigate taking the brunt of the strike. At the sound of their crackling hull, Ki'Leena turned her head to see the havoc she wrought. The frigate no longer appeared to have a stern, and the crew was scrambling for cover from the rifle fire from Hammerhead's crew.

"Rope men, go help to repair any damage!" Ki'Leena began with her following orders. "Starboard to port, ready the cannons!"

"We're not boarding them Shipmaster?" A confused man wondered.

"We will." Ki'Leena affirmed.

The Shipmaster turned the wheel to port, sailing against the wind for only moments before achieving a southern tack. They'd moved just far enough west to clear the island's shelf, and she intended to circle it. The ship of the line had picked up enough momentum that dragging the heavily damaged frigate only slowed it by a knot or two. It helped that the frigate's own sails were carrying it.

Hammerhead's crew seemed uneasy, not sure exactly what their new Shipmaster was planning. However the riflemen diligently maintained their line, successfully keeping the enemy crew at bay. A steady stream of gunshots echoed throughout the enclosure. The Steel Marrow was keeping pace, though Billy had avoided sticking too close, denying their enemy a single target to fire upon. Ki'Leena followed the coast, scanning the shoreline. She'd seen this tactic before.

Only minutes passed by the time she spotted her target. "Port side ready, aim for that schooner!"

Just as she thought, the Bloody Reds had hidden a ship on the other side of the island to allow the cannon crew an escape if things didn't turn out as planned.

"We see it Shipmaster, we only need a few more moments!" A man responded.

The Acacia skirted along the beach head as the anchored schooner grew clearer among the trees.

"Ready Shipmaster!"

Ki'Leena raised her left arm bent, readying to give the order. "Fire!" She yelled, extending it to signal any man that couldn't hear.

This time they were moving quickly enough that the smoke wasn't much of an issue, it was easy to confirm a successful strike on their target. The vessel immediately began to submerge into the shallow water after such a massive barrage.

Just as the Shipmaster began to turn her attention back to it, what she guessed to be at least a portion of their powder stores detonated on the Bloody Red frigate. The ship was now ablaze, and there wouldn't be a more opportune time to strike past this. Any later, and the crew might scatter into the sea to regroup with their comrades on the island.

"Draw your arms, prepare for boarding!" Ki'Leena shouted over the rumbling of the ship's faltering hull.

She turned the wheel starboard, intending to use the Acacia as a barricade and allow Hammerhead's crew to board. Visibility on the main deck was poor. Smoke was pluming from the lower decks, and riflemen on both sides were firing blind. As Ki'Leena brought both ships to a stop, the Steel Marrow brought its long ram crashing into what was left of the enemy frigate's stern.

Ki'Leena locked the wheel one final time, drawing her sabre in her right hand and a knife in her left with a reverse grip.

As she made her way down to the main deck, she heard a vicious snarl of a man's voice that boomed across the Acacia's main deck. ***"Hammerhead!"***

Footsteps rapidly moved closer to them, a sound almost as aggressive as the cries of a man who was clearly out for blood.

"*Where is that salty cunt!?*" He yelled once more.

The footsteps of what must've been a sizable person finally stopped with one especially heavy landing, followed shortly by a massive figure bursting from the smoke around the frigate's bowsprit.

It was... A Na'Sakka? No. While he bore a very strong resemblance, like Billy many of his features differed and his coat was a muted grey. The man wielded a sword the likes of which Ki'Leena had never seen before. The blade was nearly the length of his body, and the hilt could support at least three hands. The guard was in a chevron pattern, each side half the size of the grip.

He held it high above his head as he seemingly flew towards the Acacia's main deck, clearly intending to cleave anything unfortunate enough to be where he meant to land. As luck would have it, a man Ki'Leena actually recognized stood in his path just before the main mast.

The crewman managed to just barely block the incoming blow, but the force knocked him straight to the ground and sent his cutlass rattling across the wooden floor. His hand was bleeding, and the enemy sailor was readying a final blow.

As he was about to strike the man down, Ki'Leena's boot to the left side of his gut sent him stumbling off balance.

"Get to cover." The Shipmaster softly commanded, moving between them.

The crewman scrambled to his feet and ran away from the ensuing fight. Ki'Leena lowered her stance, leveling her sword diagonally in front of her. The hand holding the knife was at the ready behind her.

The pirate wasn't staggered for long. While both crews met with a clashing of blades and launched themselves between ships, he slowly approached her with malice in his eyes. "Give me the woman that sank my ship, and I won't paint this deck with your blood!"

"Thane Hornigold, captain of the Seadog!" Hammerhead announced from the poop deck.

While he looked to her, Ki'Leena never let her focus waver from him.

"I thought that might be you." She continued. "But it's been so long since your handsome little frigate was allowed on the shores of Aussan, I couldn't be certain without seeing your knappy hide up close."

"Do you mean to cower behind your crew you lousy fussock, or are you going to come down and make this easier for the both of us!?"

"You've got the wrong gal I'm afraid. As it happens on this fine night: You somehow managed to find yourself bested by the new girl there."

Thane turned his gaze back to Ki'Leena in that moment, his previous violent intent shifting to an even more obvious fury. He shot his glare back at Hammerhead and pointed. "In that case: When I'm done with her, I might just allow you to live as my own personal tail."

Hammerhead let out a barely audible chuckle as she stepped onto the railing and took hold of a loose, hanging rope. "Ki'Leena!" She shouted, finally getting the Shipmaster's attention. "Soften him up until I get back."

With that, the Captain swung into the blackened smoke of the Sea Dog, and Ki'Leena turned back to her opponent.

Captain Thane had already raised his sword for the first strike by the time her eyes were back on him. Knowing a man twice her size might have the strength to break her guard even without the assistance of a leap, she instead chose to deflect his attack to her right.

The Shipmaster was about to attack with her knife thinking he was open, until she realized the pommel of his sword was rapidly approaching her face. With a backstep she evaded it, but Thane was already moving into a sweeping swing from the same direction. This she was forced to roll away from, losing her hat in the process.

He was a lot quicker than one might expect, even keeping a nimble fighter like Ki'Leena on her toes. Just as she feared: All the blustering may actually be well earned.

Before Thane could followup his advance, one of his crewmen attempted to attack the Shipmaster. He came in with a thrust, which she deflected to his left with her sword swaying downward. With his back exposed to her: She stabbed her offhand knife into the right side of his neck, ran her sabre through his kidney, and finished by kicking him away to draw the blades back out of him.

She faced the Bloody Red captain with her lowered stance the moment her weapons were free. As expected, he was already swinging from his right. Against her better judgement, she decided to face the blow head-on. With a low blade she caught the attack, locking his weapon in her own hand guard. Ki'Leena moved his sword over her head, stepping under it in the same motion.

Once on the other side, she instinctively went for a stab. But Thane was ready for it. He'd actually let go of his weapon with his right hand, using it to catch her left as it came down. He turned more towards her slightly, using the motion to empower a left footed kick straight to her gut. He didn't let go of her arm though, instead her lower body flailed in the air as he held her up off the ground.

She had completely lost her breath, and was momentarily stunned by it. Captain Thane lightly tossed his sword up, catching it by the blade just above the hand guard with a reverse hold. She attempted to slash at him, but he deflected it away with the grip of his sword. As if to further prolong her delirium, he thrusted the hilt and guard straight into her chin as she hung there in his grasp.

Seeming unsatisfied with the effect, he stepped back and turned, slamming her back into the main mast. In a stroke of fortune, it almost felt as if the pain of the blow knocked the sense back into her. Somehow, she'd managed to keep hold of her weapons through it all.

When he once again suspended her in front of him, Ki'Leena swung herself up and wrapped her legs around his arm. She used the momentum to toss him away, freeing herself from his grasp. However she was still in pain, and couldn't afford to be grabbed like that again. She started running towards the poop deck hoping to attempt a new plan of attack. She clearly couldn't risk her usual defensive fighting style with an opponent that could so easily overpower her.

Thane was quick to make chase, but she actually did have an aim. As the pirate was running up behind her, Ki'Leena in one full motion stopped, turned, and threw her sabre with as much force as she could muster. He didn't have time to react, as the blade flew at a blistering speed and burrowed into his left shoulder.

The moment he drew back in pain, the Shipmaster unclasped the sheath of her kukuri knife and drew it. Instead of taking on her usual stance, she leapt towards him with a swift chop. Thane, still reeling from the sword in his shoulder, stepped back and deflected the attack. She continued to press forward, slashing, stabbing and chopping with both weapons in a fluid motion. She was sure to keep one or the other at the ready to parry if he attacked. He no longer had the advantage of reach, and she used the opportunity to push him towards her fellow crewmates who were currently gathering on the main deck.

Once again taking up the defense if only in stance, Ki'Leena let up her attack as to avoid wearing herself out. Thane held onto the hilt of his sword with his left hand, now with a forward grip. Using the other, he pulled the Shipmaster's sabre out of his shoulder. He looked around, clearly noticing that Hammerhead and Billy's crews had prevailed, and were awaiting the result of the duel.

Captain Thane wrapped his right hand around the blade of his sword a foot above the guard with a reverse grip, and raised the tip against Ki'Leena.

The Shipmaster heard muttering begin around them, comments from the crew about her own performance and the strangeness of their fighting styles.

Ki'Leena feigned an advancing attack, prompting Thane to attempt a thrust. She used the knife in her left hand to brush it to that same side. When he attempted to counter her followup attack with his good hand, he was painfully informed that's what she was aiming for. Her kukuri blade landed between his fingers, splitting the flesh of his hand.

Thane cried out in agony, attempting to move away from her. Much to his dismay, she chopped down a second time. His left forearm was her target this time. The strike caused him to finally drop his sword.

"Alright princess, that's enough." Hammerhead bemused from behind.

However, the Shipmaster didn't quite register the request. As Thane pressed both of his arms to his torso in an attempt to put pressure on both wounds, Ki'Leena chopped low, the attack landing on the outside of his left thigh. The blow caused him to drop to his knees, wailing yet again.

As Ki'Leena raised her blade to chop down onto the back of his neck, a familiar striped maroon hand caught her forearm. "Ki'Leena!" She nearly shouted, finally getting the Shipmaster's attention. "That's enough." She consoled, and let go. "He's more use to us alive."

Ki'Leena stood up straight and stepped back, taking a few deep breaths to calm herself.

"Whatever for, Cap'n?" A crewman asked.

"Two-thousand therons, of course." Hammerhead replied with a smirk.

"You plan to take my bounty, you self righteous witc..." Thane attempted to sneer, before being cut off by a swift jab across the face from Billy.

Hammerhead seemed a little surprised by the reaction.

"What? He was pissin' me off." Billy stated.

The Captain got down on one knee beside him as he attempted to get back onto his own. "Honestly Thane, I don't know yet. I can't decide if you're too talented to kill, or too talented to spare."

"Spare me so that I can what, sail for you?" Thane nearly spat the words from his mouth.

"You didn't have to sign on with the Republic to avoid ending up an enemy, blaggard." She jided.

"Save it, I'll not be lectured in ethics by the Maneater of all people."

Hammerhead's expression was unchanging, but Ki'Leena could swear she felt a raw anger emanating from her in that moment. It's certainly not a nickname she'd heard any of the Captain's friends call her.

"For someone so dead-set on opposing the Empire he'd throw all sense to the wind, you're sure quick to believe any line they feed you." Hammerhead in a sudden motion clenched her claws around his throat, staring right into his eyes. "You're not a man that has much left to lose, Thane. I'd advise you to watch your tongue before I make my decision."

She released her grip and stood up, almost as if she had a mind to leave him to the crew before she remembered something. Hammerhead drew her pistol and shot Thane in his other thigh.

"What was that for?" He cried out, as if channeling the pain through the protest.

"For tossing my Shipmaster around. I couldn't very well do it while she was showing off her fancy moves."

Ki'Leena couldn't help but catch on to the fact that Hammerhead was apparently observing the fight when she was meant to be assisting in the boarding of The Seadog.

The former Captain Thane was moved to the Acacia's brig shortly after the exchange. He received minimal treatment for his wounds, even that was only afforded at the prospect of a possible payout for his bounty.

Hammerhead had ordered a barrage of cannonfire on the island to flush out or kill the men stationed there for the ambush. The destruction of such a large portion of the forest gave Ki'Leena pause, but she made no protest given the sound logic of the strategy. Sure enough, the attack caused what was left of the crew to emerge from the brush and surrender. Nonetheless, Billy's men headed a search across the small island for any survivors... or a possible last stand.

The cannon crew were bound and lined up on the beach. While nothing had been said about it as of yet, it was obvious to anyone their fate was sealed. The only thing they were worth to the crews of the victors was some sense of justice for those lost. These were their final moments to look out at the stars and make their peace.

Indeed there were some living scattered among what was once an idyllic landscape, but if they had any plans for a counter attack they were deprived of any chance to realize it. The remains of their schooner were looted for any supplies or goods it held, of which there was a surprising amount.

As the various searches ended, Captain Hammerhead commandeered a table and chair from the encampment. She brought some of her record keeping supplies from her cabin and laid it out alongside a lit candle. Some men helped to bring a large chest from aboard. The wounded and otherwise besmirched members of the Acacia's crew were instructed to take a moment's rest nearby while they waited to be called upon.

Ki'Leena tended to the injuries of those she could, observing the process as she did. This was the first time since she'd joined them that any of the men seemed glad to be around her. A surprisingly kind soul by the name of "Sam" assisted the Shipmaster as she cared for everyone.

Before much of a wait, the Captain requested a man named John approach the table.

"Uh Cap'n..." he began as he drew near. "The men are waitin' to hear what will become of the survivors."

Hammerhead took a moment from jotting something down in one of her books to look at him directly. "The injured and matelots of the dead will have the honor of executing them. If there aren't enough to go around, favor the latter."

"Aye Cap'n." John confirmed, and left to relay the order. Saheel left the Captain's side to go with him, presumably to moderate the proceeding.

"Wounded!" Hammerhead called out. "If you can stand, line up at the table. If you can't, I'll get to you afterward."

As each man approached, Ki'Leena could hear them discuss the extent of their injuries. The Captain had opened the chest that was brought down... It was filled to the brim with therons.

Every crewman was paid on the spot for each injured body part, the value of each increased with import. Fingers, toes and even legs paid the least. Arm, shoulder and torso wounds were the most compensated.

Sam explained to the Shipmaster at her curiosity behind the reasoning: "A man can still walk on a peg, but he can't pull a rope or hold a weapon with a bad arm."

The amount surprised Ki'Leena as well. Those that were more gravely injured seemed to receive enough to leave at port and begin a new life if they desired.

This was made even more evident as Hammerhead began making her way around to those that couldn't line up. After she was finished writing in her book, she left to bring back quite the pretty sum for each of them.

"Ki'Leena..." The Captain spoke from behind, prompting the Shipmaster to stop what she was doing and turn to face her. "I'm going to go help the men collect the jewelry of the fallen, keep record. You... just keep doing what you seem to do best."

The statement did confound Ki'Leena, causing her to inquire. "Why would you take their jewelry?"

Hammerhead was only a little surprised by the question, she'd begun to become accustomed to the Shipmaster's unfamiliarity with most commonalities. She could also see how it might look quite distasteful without context.

"To pay for their funerals when we reach port, it's why they wear it." She explained.

Though she didn't seem to intend it, the Captain's deliberation was a bit cold. As if she's done this several times before. Ki'Leena supposed it was to be expected given her age, but... something about that made another notion from earlier nag at her even more.

Her train of thought was broken by the sudden sharp crackle of gunfire further down the shore.

The night dragged on, and the crews of both ships took the opportunity to rest at shore and make use of some of the acquired liquor and supplies before they were to eventually load what was left onto the ships in the morning. Friends and matelots of the dead took time to mourn and share a drink in their name.

Ki'Leena had something on her mind, though. And when Hammerhead finally retired to her cabin, she took the opportunity to follow shortly after.

The Captain was in a state of undress when she entered, wearing only her blouse and trousers. She seemed somewhat caught off guard by the Shipmaster's sudden entrance.

"You're ready to retire too, I take it?" Hammerhead wondered after sparing a glance back at her.

"Actually, uh..." Ki'Leena stammered, finding herself shockingly anxious. She closed the door behind her, clenching the knob as opposed to simply releasing it. "I wanted to ask you something."

"Of course, what do you need?" The Captain replied, turning her full attention towards her with a genuine tone the Shipmaster hadn't expected. Her usual bluster was gone, perhaps the events of the night had effected her more than she let on?

Ki'Leena took a moment while Hammerhead looked on, waiting to hear what she was after. Finally finding her words, the Shipmaster looked back up at her. "What do you want from me, exactly?"

"I'm sorry?" Hammerhead asked, not certain what the implication was.

"You hire me saying you need my skillset." Ki'Leena began. "The first thing you attempt to do is sleep with me, but then say you'd respect that I didn't want that. Then, you apparently are watching over my safety during a battle when you're meant to be assisting a crew you seem far more platonic with and even somewhat detached from..."

Hammerhead's gaze finally faltered with the realization she'd apparently let on more than she'd intended as of late.

"And don't tell me you 'just wanted to observe my performance' or some such tale. You didn't need to hide and watch me the whole time just to get an idea of that." Ki'Leena added.

The Captain peered back up at her, and did her best to explain. "*I know* we've only known each other for weeks at this point. And I know, some of my earliest interactions with you weren't entirely... innocent. But I have to admit: Since then, I've taken a bit of a... shine, to you."

"... Why?" Ki'Leena wondered, making no attempt to hide her bewilderment.

Hammerhead was quite a bit more reserved than usual, she wasn't accustomed to sharing any sort of deep-seated emotion with others. Even those she was closer to, she hadn't conversed with in such a way for quite some time.

"Despite how little time we've shared, it's obvious to me that you're... different, from most I've met. Kind. Gentle, even. To the point that when you shared your past, I frankly found it very difficult to believe. It was really only the details I already knew myself that made me accept it as honesty."

Ki'Leena finally let go of the door and began stepping forward as Hammerhead continued.

"And... I've enjoyed the short time we've had. You're pleasant to be around. Unlike most, I don't get the impression this is a path you tread at all lightly. So, I suppose I was worried... about you..." Finally, some semblance of the Captain's usual boisterousness returned. "That's it, I don't **want** anything from you. It's not some **long play** on my part."

Hammerhead hadn't noticed just how close Ki'Leena had gotten to her while she divulged her true intentions. For the first time in quite some time, she was feeling a bit flustered herself. This was the first moment they'd simply stood so close next to each other with no distractions, and she was somewhat surprised to realize that the Shipmaster was actually a fair bit taller than she was.

Ki'Leena stared down at her in silence, contemplating precisely how she wanted to respond to what she'd just heard. She knew how she felt... she just didn't know if acting upon it was the wisest decision.

Slowly, she raised her hand and began to gently run her fingers across the otherworldly woman's cheek. Her skin was extremely smooth, soft in a way Ki'Leena could scarcely comprehend.

Hammerhead was taken aback, not quite used to being the one to receive such a forward gesture. Though she certainly made no protest as the dark skinned woman's hand moved further along and she felt a gentle touch run through her hair. Her legs seemed to grow weaker, softly stumbling back onto the desk that was behind her.

She wasn't entirely certain when Ki'Leena's other arm ended up around her waist... Their lips meeting however: That was something incredibly difficult to mistake.

Made in the USA
Columbia, SC
22 December 2022